The Greedy Dog

Based on a story by Aesop

Retold by Alex Frith

Illustrated by
Francesca di Chiara

Reading consultant: Alison Kelly
Roehampton University

Dog was always hungry.

One day, he trotted
to the market.

He spotted a bone.

"Look at that bone," Dog barked.

"I want it!"

No one was looking.

Greedy Dog grabbed
the bone.

Then he
ran away.

9

Soon, he came to
a river.

Dog looked into
the water.

He saw
another dog!

"That dog has a bigger bone," he thought.

"I want it!"

He growled at the dog
in the water.

The dog in the water growled back.

He barked at the dog
in the water.

The bone fell out of his
mouth.

Splash!

The other dog vanished.

20

"Oh no!" barked Dog.

"Now I have no bone
at all."

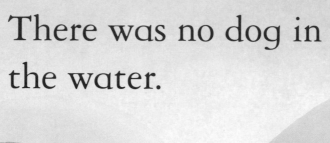

There was no dog in
the water.

It was Greedy Dog's
reflection all along.

PUZZLES

Puzzle 1

Can you spot the differences between these two pictures?

There are six to find.

Puzzle 2

Look at the pictures and put them in order:

A

B

C

D

Puzzle 3

Find these things in the picture:

bee	fish	house
river	dog	hill

Puzzle 4

Choose the best word to match each picture.

sad   hungry

growling   happy

About the story

The Greedy Dog is one of Aesop's Fables, a collection of stories first told in Ancient Greece around 4,000 years ago. The stories always have a "moral" (a message or lesson) at the end. The moral in this story is...

...don't be greedy!

Answers to puzzles

Puzzle 1

Puzzle 2

C   A   D   B

Puzzle 3

house

hill

bee

dog

river

fish

Puzzle 4

growling   sad   hungry   happy

Designed by Caroline Spatz
Series editor: Lesley Sims
Series designer: Russell Punter

First published in 2012 by Usborne Publishing Ltd.,
Usborne House, 83-85 Saffron Hill, London EC1N 8RT, England.
www.usborne.com Copyright © 2012 Usborne Publishing Ltd.